Today is the Day to Run Away

Written by Denise Rogers
Illustrated by Paula Green

Big Toe Publishing
Burnaby, BC
Canada
bigtoepublishing.com

Library and Archives Canada Cataloguing in Publication

Rogers, Denise, 1953–

    Today is the day to run away / written by Denise Rogers ; illustrated by Paula Green.

ISBN 978-0-9867160-0-3

    I. Green, Paula (Paula D.), 1955– II. Title.

PS8635.O426T63 2010   jC813'.6   C2010-906400-3

Design and layout by Vancouver Desktop Publishing Centre
Author's photograph by The Artona Group Inc.

Just two short weeks before her eighth birthday in 2008, Cassidy Leigh Briggs was diagnosed with Hepatocellular Carcinoma, a very rare pediatric tumor. This diagnosis was the beginning of a tremendous battle that Cassidy fought bravely and determinedly until her death on January 11th, 2010.

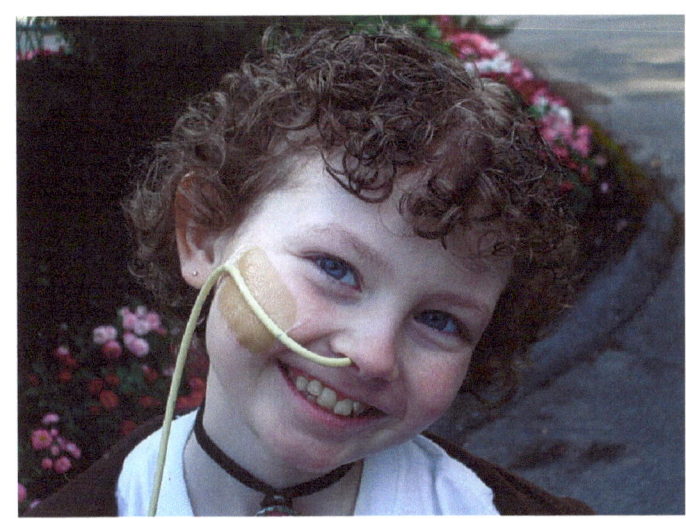

Cassidy had a dream to make the world a better place. She used every experience as an opportunity to make things better. Through Cassidy's incredible determination and amazing spirit, she became an inspiration for all those around her.

Before her death, Cassidy was working to make life better for the patients at the BC Children's Hospital. During many of her numerous stays at the hospital, she noticed that there was not enough for the children to do there as they worked at healing. Cassidy devised a plan to campaign the community for crafts for the hospital. Unfortunately, Cassidy passed away before her dream was a reality.

However, Cassidy's friends, schoolmates, teachers and family wanted to make Cassidy's dream a reality.

Get Involved
If you, your school or your organization would like to get involved, please forward donations directly to:

BC Children's Hospital Foundation
938 West 28th Avenue
Vancouver, BC V5Z 4H4

To my husband Stephen who is my greatest supporter.

—Denise Rogers

To Lexi Diane Hutchison.

—Paula Green

Big Right Toe woke up and decided that
today was the day to run away.

Wiggling and giggling, the little toes woke up, one by one. They turned and looked at the big toes; first the right, then the left. The left one was still sleeping.

"Big Right, is this the day?" they asked.

"Yes!" exclaimed Big Right. "Today is the day to run away."

"Tell us again where you want to go." They all wanted to know.

"Well, I've never seen Europe so we could start there," Big Right replied. "Oh to see the Eiffel Tower, Big Ben or the Leaning Tower of Pisa. That would be wonderful."

"That's a long way to go to run away,"
squealed the little toes. "Couldn't it be
somewhere closer? And . . . and . . . and . . .
after shoe shopping today we're all going to
the beach. Don't you love the squishy, mushy
sand and the water running up, and jumping
on the waves? What about running away
tomorrow? Please, please, please?"

Big Right thought for a minute and said,
"No. *Today* is the day to run away. Pizza in
Pisa is looking pretty good right now."

Then Big Right looked up, way up, and added, "Mom is coming. Everyone quiet now while we slide into our slippers."

"Oooo," the little toes said one by one. "We love slippers. They are so soft, and they have bunnies on them. And we can look up and still see out."

Big Left stretched and said, "Why do you want to run away today?"

Big Right harrumphed, "We don't have any
fun. We get covered up by a sock and stuffed
in a shoe or a runner. Don't you want to do
something different?"

"Maybe. But, first we need to go shopping
for new shoes for the birthday party,"
explained Big Left. "Besides wouldn't we get
covered by socks and shoes in Europe too?"

Big Right replied, "But Europe would still
be different."

The little toes squealed in delight and said, "We love red shoes . . . candy apple red. Please let them be red."

Big Right grumbled, "What's wrong with the same old shoes? We wear the same old slippers. We *can't* go shoe shopping because *today is the day to run away!*"

The little toes gulped. They didn't like it when Big Right was unhappy. What would happen now?

Big Left looked over and said, "We need you to cooperate just a little longer. Breakfast is over, and now it's time for a bath, and we get to play in the bubbles."

The little toes twitched in excitement. "We love bubbles."

Dried off and sitting in sandals, all the toes marched down the street to the shoe store.

The big, tall man was helping find shoes. "Put a sock on first," he said, "so you can try on these shoes."

"It's still summer, and it's too hot for socks," complained Big Right. "Today *really* is the day to run away."

Big Left calmly said, "It's only for a few minutes. Take a deep breath. Here they come."

"Oh," said the little toes. "It's dark in here. Thank goodness we have each other to hold on to . . . Hey, we did it! It's not so bad, Big Right."

The first pair of shoes was too tight and the same with the next pair and the next pair and the next pair.

"Ouch," said all the toes.

"See, I told you we should have run away," said Big Right.

"My," said the big, tall man. "Your feet must have grown over the summer. We'd better measure them." Then off he went to get a bigger size.

"That was painful," said all the toes. "Being pushed is not fun!"

Finally they found a pair that fit. "But . . . but . . . but . . ." cried the little toes. "They aren't red."

"I like red shoes better too!" Big Right declared. "We should have run away today."

Big Left didn't know what to do. All the toes were very upset now, and Big Left tried to soothe them as they walked down the street. They stepped off the curb and suddenly a car was speeding toward them!

Big Right scrunched to a halt and curled around the curb making everyone stop. The little toes screamed, "Big Right, you saved the day! Thank you, thank you!"

Big Right smiled thinking how much the little toes had helped too, all of them, working together.

Then off they went to the beach. Today was *not* the day to run away after all!

THE END

About the Author

Denise wrote *Today is the Day to Run Away* after she broke one of her toes. It was such a painful experience she wondered what her toe would have said about it.

While creating art with children through a number of programs for the City of Burnaby, BC, Canada she was inspired to write children's stories. Previously, she had edited professional journals and company newsletters, designed training manuals and contributed to a column in the *Burnaby NewsLeader*. Her background is in training and development and adult education. For more information about Denise visit bigtoepublishing.com

About the Illustrator

Paula Green spent four years at the University of Alaska studying art in different media, but art has been a part of her life since she could hold a brush. Oil painting in particular has been her forté and she also has taken courses in graphic design. Paula spent 28 years in retail merchandising but has recently taken on a new challenge in art through illustrating children's books. Paula can be contacted at pauladgreen@yahoo.com

Teacher/Parent Activities

Foot Mobile

Materials:
Construction paper, markers, scissors, one-hole punch, string, tape, cardboard roll (from wax paper or aluminum foil)

- Trace bare feet onto construction paper.
- Cut out traced feet patterns.
- Punch one hole through the heel of each foot pattern.
- Cut one piece of string for each foot pattern. Vary length of string pieces.
- Thread one end of string through hole in each foot pattern and tie knot.
- Tie other end of string around cardboard roll and knot.
- Tie a piece of string around cardboard roll at the point where mobile is balanced. Suspend mobile by attaching other end of string to a place (i.e., the ceiling) that allows mobile to move freely.

Foot Painting

Materials:
Non toxic paint, roll of paper, paint brush for each colour or tray for paint

- Use paint brush to paint sole of foot or dip foot or toes into paint and paint a picture or create foot prints.
- Paint geometric shapes with feet.
- Use a different paint colour for each child. Then have children walk on long piece of paper to create a personal trail. When paint is dry, children can take turns walking in each other's footprints.

Foot Math

- Trace feet onto different coloured construction paper and cut out.
- Sort feet according to size or colour. For older children number footprints from one to ten. Have children arrange foot prints in numerical order.
- Have children use their feet or traced feet to measure the length of an object. Record how many of each child's feet it takes to measure the object.

Drama

- Enact the story: ten children will each be a different toe while the remaining children will be the rest of the foot.
- Make toe puppets to tell the story. Use felt, construction paper, popsicle sticks, etc.
- Make a felt board story.